La Brea Avenue
Los Angeles, CA 90016

BALDWIN HILLS BRANCH – JULY 2016

P9-CRE-458

USE YOUR IMAGINATION

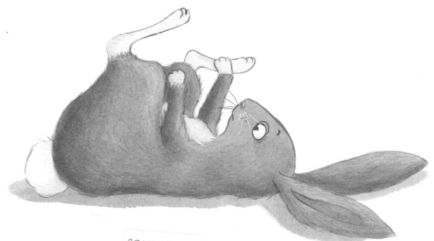

221419527
XZ
O

Nicola O'Byrne

nosy
crow

An imprint of Candlewick Press

One day, Rabbit
was feeling bored.
"I wish **something** would happen,"
he said.

"Excuse me,"

said a voice. "May I help?"

It was Wolf.

"Well, maybe . . ." said Rabbit. "I'm bored."

"Why don't we write a story?"
said Wolf. "I am a librarian, you know,
and librarians know **a lot**
about stories."

"You don't look like a librarian," said Rabbit.
"What **big ears** you have!"

"All the better for **listening to stories** with, my dear," said Wolf.

"And what **big eyes** you have!" said Rabbit.

"All the better for **reading** with, my dear," said Wolf.

"Hmmm, I'm sure I've heard something like that before," said Rabbit.

"Never mind that," said Wolf quickly.
"Let's get on with the story."

"But how do we start?"
asked Rabbit.

"You need to

USE YOUR IMAGINATION!

That means using *words* and pictures to create a story," explained Wolf. "And, of course, there's really only **one** way to begin a story. . . .

ONCE UPON A TIME!"

"But what is our story going to be about?"
asked Rabbit.

"Well," said Wolf, **"USE YOUR IMAGINATION."**

"Space rockets!" cried Rabbit. "BIG explosions!
And bananas. We need LOTS of bananas!"

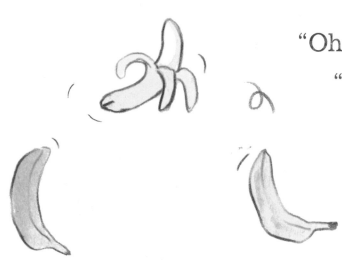

"Oh, I don't think so," said Wolf.
"What we need is a
fairy tale, something to
really sink your teeth into.
And, of course, all fairy tales
need a bad guy."

"What about a mouse?"
asked Rabbit.

"I was thinking about
something **bigger**,"
said Wolf.

"An **elephant**!" cried Rabbit.

"How about something
medium-size?"
said Wolf quickly.

"I know! What about **you**?"
asked Rabbit.

"Now, **that's**
a good idea,"
said Wolf.

"What next?" asked Rabbit.

"Well, of course, we need a hero," said Wolf.

"Me, me, me!" said Rabbit.

"What a great idea!" said Wolf.

"But what will I wear?" said Rabbit.

"Oh, it doesn't matter much," said Wolf. **"USE YOUR IMAGINATION."**

"A **SPACE SUIT**!" cried Rabbit.

"Or a pirate hat! Or . . . what about a little red cape?"

"Oh, you probably don't need a costume," said Wolf, smiling.

"But where does this story happen?" asked Rabbit.

"USE YOUR IMAGINATION," said Wolf.

"That's a tricky one," said Rabbit.
"What do you think?"

"I was thinking of somewhere . . . tree-y," said Wolf.

"Oh, what about a forest?" squeaked Rabbit.

"Now, that's a good idea," said Wolf.

Rabbit felt very proud. "We've got a bad guy, a hero,
AND a forest," he said. "Is the story going to start soon?"

"Oh, yes," said Wolf, grinning. "The story starts . . .

RIGHT NOW!"

"I don't like this story at all!" panted Rabbit

as Wolf

chased after

him.

"Really?" snarled Wolf.
"Well, don't worry.
We're nearly
at the
end."

"Isn't using your

IMAGINATION

a wonderful thing?"

"Now **that** was
a good idea,"
said Rabbit.

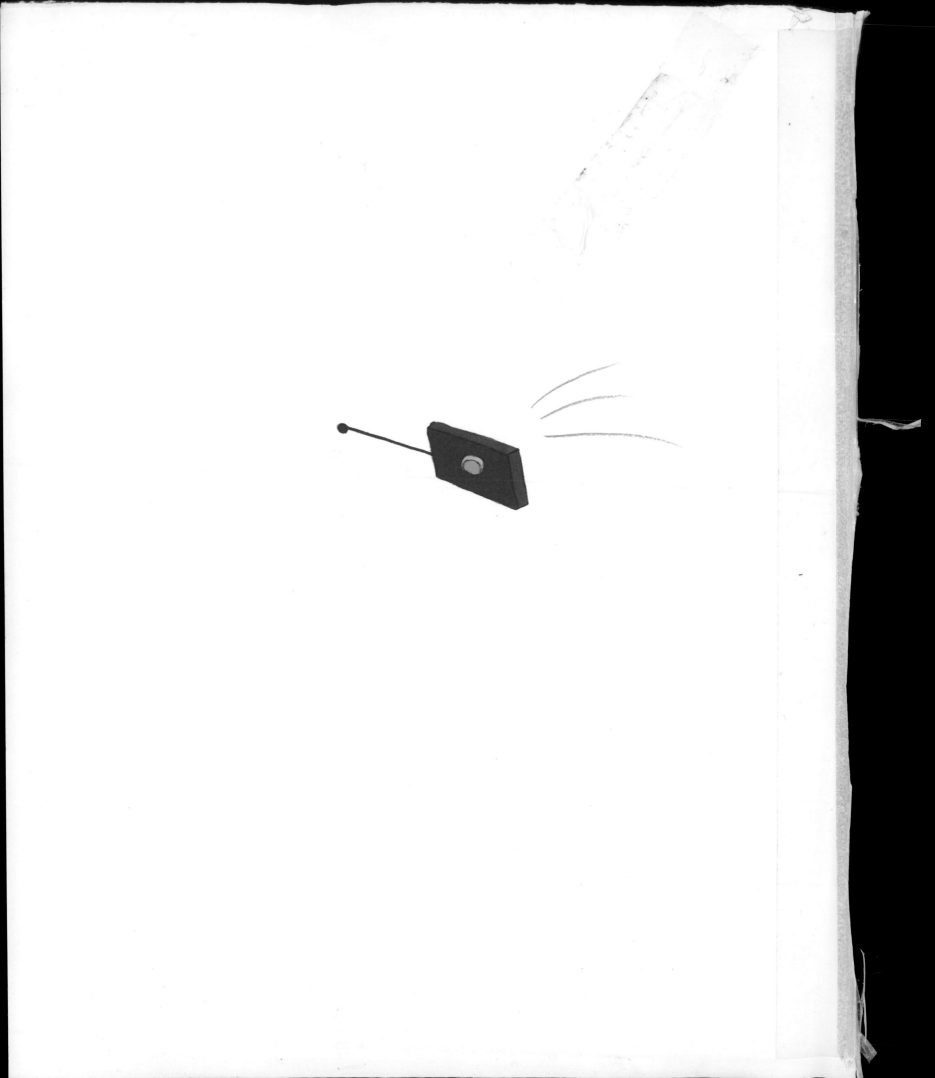

Rabbit did.

"This *isn't* a good idea **AT ALL**," said Wolf.

Rabbit grinned.
"Well, don't worry, we're nearly at the **end.**"

5, 4, 3, 2, 1...

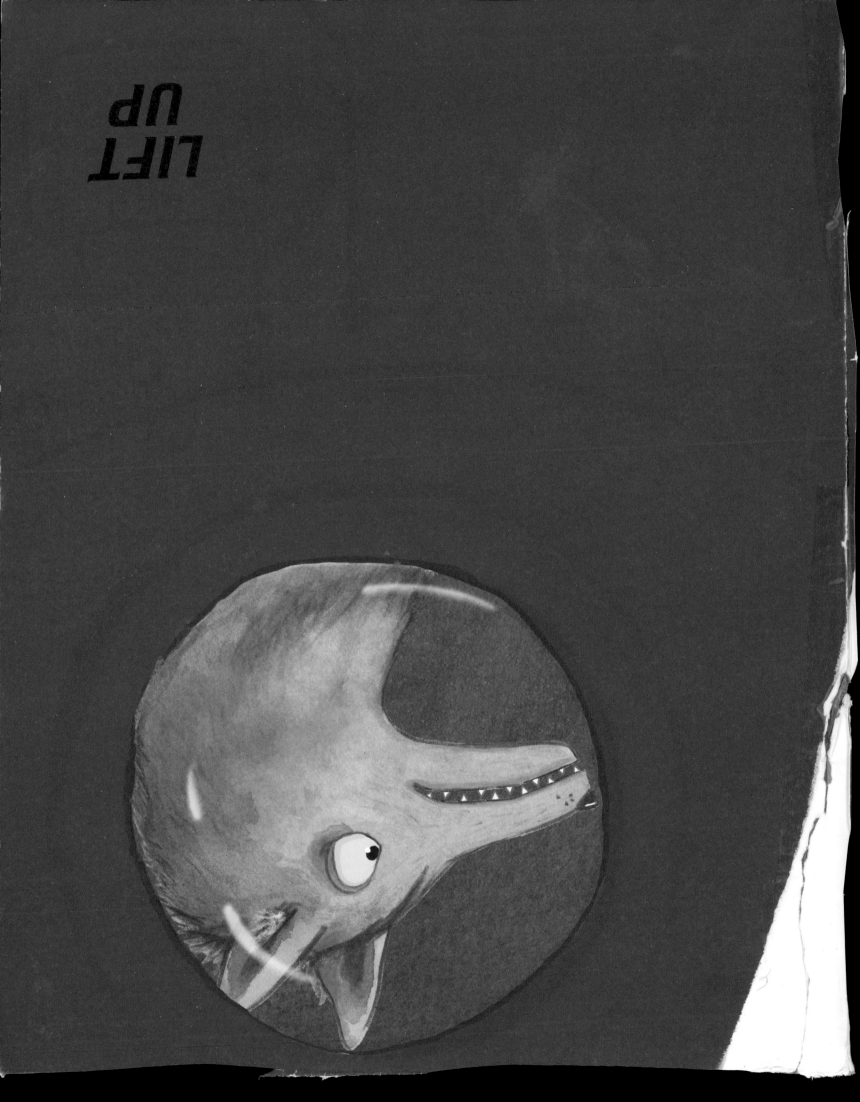

LIFT UP